D0543421

KIRKLEES LIBRARIES

THE ADVENTURES OF MR TOAD

KENNETH GRAHAME'S
THE
WIND
IN THE
WILLOWS

AS RETOLD BY
TOM MOORHOUSE

ILLUSTRATED BY
DAVID ROBERTS

OXFORD
UNIVERSITY PRESS

One day I was sitting outside my home, Toad Hall, and reading a map. Well, that's what I was **meant** to be doing. Really I was making up songs about myself. Like this one:

Ahem.
(That's me clearing my throat before singing.)

I'm the magnificent,
wise Mr Toad,
the finest of creatures
you ever have knowed!
The handsomest fellow,
the cleverest too –
the best Toad around,
yes of course that is true.

A cheery voice called, 'Hello there!' from the river.

And who did I see but Ratty and Mole in their boat!

'What splendid luck!' I cried. 'You can come
for an outing in my new favourite thing:
my shiny yellow caravan!'

All afternoon we rolled down green country lanes,
and that evening I delighted Mole and Ratty
with my wonderful songs.

But we had barely set off the next day when
poop poop! a motor car roared past
and barged our caravan into a ditch!

'You scoundrels!' shouted Ratty,
jumping up and down.

But all I heard was the beautiful sound of the car's horn.

Poop *poop!*

And now I was done with silly caravans. I wanted a car.
A **real** one!

Ahem.

I'm the magnificent, wise Mr Toad,
the finest of drivers around on the road.
My goggles and gloves make me look rather dashing.
But I'm never quite sure why my cars keep on . . .
crashing.

Ratty, Mole, and Badger told me to stop buying cars.

'Take those ridiculous things off him,' Badger ordered,
and Ratty sat on me while Mole took away my goggles
and driving gloves. 'Now off to his room, and he can
stay there until he stops this nonsense.'

But they couldn't stop me driving in my bedroom!
And when I was bored I got dressed, tied my sheets
together, and sneaked out of the window.

Ahem.

I am the cunning,
and bold Mr Toad,
the best escape artist
the world ever knowed!
I outwitted old Badger,
and Ratty, and Mole,
and now I'm about to
go out for a stroll!

In the town I spied a big, beautiful motor car . . .
And nobody was nearby.

'Well, looking can't hurt,' I thought.

But somehow I found both my hands
on the steering wheel.

'I wonder if this sort of car starts easily . . .

. . . oh, it does!'

Ahem.
I'm the incredibly swift Mr Toad,
the speediest creature you ever have knowed!
I'm Toad at my highest, I'm Toad on a roll,
going faster, and faster, and losing control until...

CRASH!

The car was a wreck.

It was ~~toad~~ towed away.

And I was thrown into prison.

Sniff.

I'm the forlorn and alone Mr Toad,
the sorriest creature
  you ever have knowed.
Oh, intelligent Ratty,
  and sensible Mole,
and Badger, you wonderful,
  faithful old soul:
I wish I had
  heeded your words
  when I could,
  but now it's too
late
  and I'm
locked up
  for good.

The jailer's kind daughter took pity on me and brought me some clothes.

Disguised as a washerwoman I walked right out of the prison. I caught a fast train and escaped down the tracks.

Then I rode a grey horse all
the way home to my friends.

Ahem.
I'm the magnificent,
daredevil Toad,
the most adventurous creature
you ever have knowed.
I escaped from the prison
and now I am free.
What a wonderful feeling
it is to be me!

But back home Ratty, Mole, and Badger gave me solemn looks and told me their terrible news. While I was away the stoats and weasels from Wildwood took Toad Hall! And they've locked it up tight and are guarding the gates!

Sniff.
Oh, what a miserable,
unhappy Toad:
the Wildwooder weasels
have taken my home!
I've been such a fool
and I've lost all my hope,
now my lovely Toad Hall
is filled right up with . . .

STOATS.

'Cheer up, Toady, I'll tell you
a great secret,' said Badger.
'There's an underground
passage that leads up to
Toad Hall. We'll sneak
in together and sort
those Wildwooders out!'

So that night, armed to the
teeth, we crept up the tunnel.

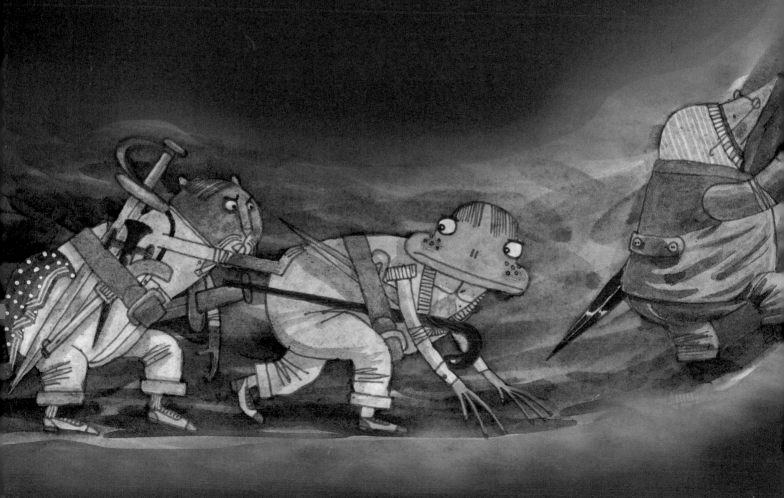

Ahem.
(Singing very quietly in case
the weasels hear me.)

I'm the courageous
and brave Mr Toad,
(I'm a little bit scared
but I'm sure that won't show).

We burst into Toad Hall, brandishing our weapons.

With Badger's stout cudgel,

and Mole's awful war-cries,

and Ratty's grim face,

and my blood-curdling Toad-whoops, we scared the pesky stoats and weasels right out of my house!

I held a big banquet to celebrate, inviting the best
animals from all around. My guests told me
how clever I was to defeat the Wildwooders.

'Sing us a song, Toady!' they cried.

But I have learned my lesson. I won't sing prideful songs
about myself any more. Well . . . maybe just one.

Ahem.

I am the happiest, luckiest Toad,
with the three best of friends that I ever have knowed.
We live by the river and laugh in the sun.
And now with this song, my adventures are . . . **done!**

OXFORD
UNIVERSITY PRESS

Great Clarendon Street, Oxford OX2 6DP

Oxford University Press is a department of the University of Oxford.
It furthers the University's objective of excellence in research, scholarship,
and education by publishing worldwide. Oxford is a registered trade mark of
Oxford University Press in the UK and in certain other countries

The moral rights of the author and illustrator have been asserted

Database right Oxford University Press (maker)

First published in 2014

First published in paperback in 2015

Text copyright © Tom Moorhouse 2014

Illustrations copyright © David Roberts 2012, 2014

All rights reserved. No part of this publication may be reproduced,
stored in a retrieval system, or transmitted, in any form or by any means,
without the prior permission in writing of Oxford University Press,
or as expressly permitted by law, or under terms agreed with the appropriate
reprographics rights organization. Enquiries concerning reproduction
outside the scope of the above should be sent to the Rights Department,
Oxford University Press, at the address above

You must not circulate this book in any other binding or cover
and you must impose this same condition on any acquirer

British Library Cataloguing in Publication Data

Data available

ISBN: 978-0-19-273867-7 (Hardback)

ISBN: 978-0-19-273868-4 (Paperback)

1 3 5 7 9 10 8 6 4 2

Printed in China

Paper used in the production of this book is a natural,
recyclable product made from wood grown in sustainable forests.
The manufacturing process conforms to the environmental
regulations of the country of origin.

For Helen Mortimer and Sarah Darby
—D.R.

For Edward and Beth
—T.M.